About the Author

The author is a thirty-five-year-old woman with a two-year-old daughter. A qualified psychotherapist who directs her professional attention to families including children with special needs and disabilities. She has a Ph.D. degree and two Masters', spent a few years in Switzerland where she acquired her MBA. A resident, of the ancient and beautiful city of St. Petersburg, Russia. And she believes that love can give the most intense emotions possible.

Jo

Klena Koroleva

Jo

Olympia Publishers
London

www.olympiapublishers.com
OLYMPIA PAPERBACK EDITION

Copyright © **Klena Koroleva 2020**

The right of Klena Koroleva to be identified as author of this work has been asserted in accordance with sections 77 and 78 of the Copyright, Designs and Patents Act 1988.

All Rights Reserved

No reproduction, copy or transmission of this publication may be made without written permission.
No paragraph of this publication may be reproduced, copied or transmitted save with the written permission of the publisher, or in accordance with the provisions of the Copyright Act 1956 (as amended).

Any person who commits any unauthorised act in relation to this publication may be liable to criminal prosecution and civil claims for damage.

A CIP catalogue record for this title is available from the British Library.

ISBN: 978-1-78830-704-8

This is a work of fiction.
Names, characters, places and incidents originate from the writer's imagination. Any resemblance to actual persons, living or dead, is purely coincidental.

First Published in 2020

**Olympia Publishers
Tallis House
2 Tallis Street
London
EC4Y 0AB**

Printed in Great Britain

Dedication

To strange and amazing Jo. More…

To my beloved mama. Thanks for believing in me. You are the best!

I'd like to thank people without whom this book would never be published in the English language. Vera Koroleva and John Burchmore, thank you so much for spending many, many hours translating this book.

If you are thirsty you use a glass of water or the whole ocean?

Part 1

Chapter 1

…And there she sat on her cushioned wooden throne
Pale skin and cold eyes.
Strength of life and memories passing.
Succumbing weight making her shoulders weep.
And there she sat, with gathered hands,
palms surrounded by her ten-fingered army.
There she was all alone, just waiting on her throne
Waiting for life and leaning back gazing at the sky
for there was no roof. Heads being held high.
Often in contempt for being scared and lonely.
Too often mistreated by wind and water.
Too often abused by loneliness and fire.
And, what else would she condone on that wooden throne.
Misunderstood on her cushioned throne, with killer legs and weeping shoulders.
Heads rolled like thoughts before pikes of pain and a hurricane.
Words not meant but being scared and alone.

But there was no roof above her throne and her feeling were made of stone.
And on that wooden throne she sat all alone.
Starlight of the night and the moon kissed her cheeks and made her stand.
Holding hands and falling stars, warmth of love and unending night.
Beauty of life in all its delight...

*

Sasha's dream appeared repeatedly, it seemed to her what she saw was like a haze, she heard something but could not understand from whom the words came, she felt her hand was being touched by somebody, and then she woke up as she had done on previous nights.

"But where is your hand?" Sasha muttered, barely audibly.

Hardly opening her eyes whilst still in bed, it was light in the room already, so it was not possible to fall asleep again. Sasha stretched to reach her mobile on the floor. There were no messages or any calls, *"although who would send messages at eight in the morning?* She thought, *because everything has changed.*

For a few months now, Sasha could not avoid her thoughts even during the night. Sleeplessness, strange night dreams, headaches, she was drowning, and she had no energy to fight this situation. It was progressively getting worse.

For two days now, she felt she had an urgent need to take a drill and make a hole in her brain, in the part where these thoughts originated. They tortured her for days not allowing sleep at all for the last two nights. They burst into her mind unbearably often, bringing about crushing pain in her breasts, she was thinking continuously and there were no tears. She promised not to cry any more. But it did not help her. She was sitting for hours in front of the screen and watching soap operas, but she had another picture in her mind.

Three weeks ago, there was no place for strong emotion in her life, it was daily routine. She accepted a long time ago a life without love, "having been compensated by insults and disappointments." Life was going on, and her motto was, *"I have to do this,"* and she looked like a gloomy battered pony who was going around in a circus with a cart full of rubbish, having already forgotten why he was doing it but just continued to move only by habit.

In those days, everything was going in the wrong direction. She lost a job connected with a project, in which, for the last three years she was fully immersed, so she has to be alone with herself. After many years, unexpectedly, she had time on her hands, but she was not ready for this situation. It scared her. The days became unbearably long. These days she was driving around the city aimlessly, she invented something to do in order to avoid her thoughts. She constantly sought to understand what had happened. Pony was kicked out of the circle and they had not indicated the direction in which to travel.

Five days later she was so exhausted that it became obvious she needs to take flight immediately. In the past she made these sorts of decision regularly. *"If you don't know what to do, take a plane."* She thought to herself.

That morning Sasha went to her favourite cafe," called Happiness." She likes it not because of what it was called. This is a strange name for a small but always crowded cafe in the centre of the Megapolis.

Happiness demands silence, solitude and your loved one. Sasha always visited this place alone, ordering the same coffee beverage and sitting at the same table with two chairs, but the view of the square from the window is amazing.

On the other side of the square, you could see a magnificent cathedral, which, by its construction, brought back memories of her beloved eternal City-Rome. Almost looming over the square, above one of four corners of this cathedral, rose a tall column, seemingly fragile when compared to others with no capping that made it less weighty. Two Bronze Angels with closely folded wings on their backs, almost convulsively squeezed this apparently weightless column and gazed with wide opened eyes at the sky.

"They are gripping so tightly for fear of flying away" Sasha thought to herself, *"how frenzied they squeezed the seemingly weightless column, as if they don't want to ascend into the sky. They are afraid... afraid of the unknown, having just become Angels, they are afraid to forget this world of which they were recently apart, where perhaps their children and lovers still live. That world does not belong any more to them, but it retains and pulls back, so strange-to be frightened of flying away."* Sasha shrugged, still lost in her thoughts, *"all cathedrals are built by mankind, and mankind are predestined to fear".*

A telephone call interrupted her thoughts. It was her mum, she offered to fly her to Belgium for a couple of weeks."

Change your location and you might be distracted from your situation, she claimed

There can be no argument about this and no energy to be against this proposal.

"I will come in a week, do not worry." Sasha said.

But this was not the end of the conversation as her mother, out of nowhere, brought up the subject of her finding someone.

"Have you met someone nice yet?" she asked.

"No," Sasha replied.

"Oh, well why not try a dating site, you could always meet at a café for and chat, you never know you might become attached and fall in love."

Sasha explained to her mother that she goes to a café alone in Petersburg and going to one alone in Belgium would be no different, but her mother was not listening and didn't change her attitude towards this.

So now, here she is, looking at a photo of a man. His location, Belgium. He had huge dark amber eyes that captivated her, but she sensed that he held many secrets and his heart was closed off, yet, those eyes, the attraction she felt towards him and the more she stared, the more she was falling. He had a simple name — Jo — and he looked a bit Spanish with brutal, tanned skin. His hair was short, not soft, almost black, and a neatly trimmed black beard.

Lightly coloured eyes are like different cocktails on the bar menu. Light blue, "Mojito", amber, Whisky, green apple, "Margarita".

All ingredients are clear. But dark eyes reminded her of "Long Island". You can never identify, if you drink this one, what it contains, so you are not capable of foreseeing the after-effects, tears, euphoria, and craziness. Therefore, reaction is unpredictable each time. Perhaps, these unknowns attracted her. Power of which she could not and did not want to resist. She always wanted to experience this power. Although, she was not ready for this.

She feels very strongly, that if she gets into a relationship with this person, it will either destroy her, or she will be in heaven. Sasha chose him. He gave her freedom with no obligation, and she appreciated that. He never asked her why she did not reply for hours or what she was busy with.

A week later and she was in Belgium, she could feel the warmth of the sun on her skin, but no matter how warm it was, she still felt chills with the thought of the events of this evening, as this will be the first meeting with the man with the dark amber eyes, she just had to hope that she didn't stare into them for too long and lose herself completely.

Chapter 2

It is now three a.m. and she has already got thirty messages in messenger, and they seemed to keep coming. The evening passed by very quickly, he took her home, looked into her eyes intently and smiled. She realised that probably from now on her life was divided into two parts. Before meeting him, and now. The only thing she did not know then, that after him there was to be a third part.

That the very first evening they decided to have dinner in a steak house found on their route. Sasha carefully watched how Jo was moving tissues and cutlery around to get them in order. How he very slowly poured sauce on to the plate near the steak. Then placed the course salt on to the left side, cut a piece of butter and together with greenery put on the edge of plate. Next the vegetables, paprika, carrots cooked in sweet sauce transferred from bowl to the plate, first to Sasha and then himself. Meat was perfect. It was juicy meat with blood. At the end of dinner Jo said something to the waitress who then soon returned with two small glasses containing an amber coloured liquid. It was Sherry. As Jo explained, you need only to consume alcoholic liquid in which there are no additional ingredients, pure drinks, Whisky, Sherry, Porto. Sherry should only be amber in colour. The red one was too sweet. After dinner he told Sasha about his family.

"My grandfather moved to Spain from the Christian part of Lebanon. My father's name was George. I have always said that my father was Spanish. If I indicated that he was from Lebanon I would be a marked man. My father came to Belgium and met my mother in the cafe at the hotel. I had already told you this story. I was born nine months later. Then in five years, Anne was born and three years later Tanya was born. Two years later my father died. I was happy to have known him whereas I regret that my sisters were too young to get to know him properly. My father opened his own restaurant in Antwerp and my mother worked there. I still keep photos of the opening day of this restaurant and of the Visitors Book containing reviews and thanks. It's a pity that we lost everything after my father's death. My father's occupation concerned investment and logistics. He dreamed of creating a company with me. And when I launched this company, I called it 'King George', but the new owners of the company renamed it. My mother isn't happy that I don't want children but I have always reminded her that my sisters can bring many grandchildren. I know exactly what it means to raise a child. I am not ready to go through it again. I started to work at an early age because my mum had no money with which to pay my college fees. I had the first experience with women when I was fifteen. I liked to joke that only men who have a small size say that it's not important."

If somebody had asked beforehand about her ideal man, she would certainly describe him. For the first time in her life all the pieces came together.

"You are strange and amazing," she likes to repeat this to herself every day, with a smile. For a long time, she had not smiled so sincerely and freely. She had not felt so alive for ages, and she had forgotten how to be happy. He helped her to breathe again. She loved to talk to him, her days became brighter and complete. It was like a breath of fresh air.

They discussed things like, poetry and the performance of Macbeth, people's fears and the nature of human actions.

She could repeatedly re-read his thoughts in Viber as if she was reading amazing stories from several different authors. Their discussions about important issues were argued until they had arrived at a conclusion. His words sounded stricter when her personal matters were talked about. Her comfort was his concern. He scolded her about her eating habits and for the absence of sporting activity in her life. For example.

He said, "The way you have your legs crossed under the table is unhealthy."

And for her attitude to work and life in general. In the last ten years, she had had two husbands, neither of which were ideal, but this guy, after only knowing him for only a week, had become her ideal man.

"Hm, hm," he would say, rather often when he was surprised by something that other people did not notice and next moment, he always slightly lifted his shoulders. She had got to love his 'hm, hm.'

You could understand his thoughts from this simple sound. His opinions were absolutely different from those of other people. He said that often, other people don't like to communicate with him. Nobody wants to hear the uncomfortable truth about themselves and nobody wants to accept the truth. The necessities of life are such that people have to live in this way.

"We only have one life and it is best to try to be happy," said Jo.

And Sasha, for the first time in her life tried to become happy, firstly for Jo, and then for herself.

She knew nothing about him except what he had told her. He was of average height, had a beautifully toned body and this meant that he had taken good care of himself — spent enough time in the gym. Thirty-three years old, Jonathan, with last syllable stressed. But he always called himself Jo.

He owns his own business, in the customs field. He owns a house, several apartments in Brussels, motorcycle and a yacht, lives with his sister, bought a separate house for his mum, well - travelled and spends money freely.

Those were only bare facts, but Sasha wasn't concerned about any of this, she didn't even ask his surname or for photos of any of his possessions that had been mentioned as confirmation. All of these things are like ballast, which pulls down, but she wanted only to go up.

Chapter 3

After their second meeting yesterday in the cinema, followed by dinner in a cosy restaurant, Sasha asked what his favourite time had been. She was waiting for him to say that his best moments were when they were kissing, hugging and smiling. But what he said, was that he liked the moment when she had taken her head off his shoulders, looked at him and smiled.

"You thought that I hadn't noticed this." He said.

She was discouraged by his reply as she wasn't used to people noticing such small things.

"I can see how you hold your fork and notice that your blood vessels are slightly oxygen deficient. Because of permanent stress, your shoulders are tense. Your facial skin is dry resulting from insufficient intake of water. Please start to think about taking more care of yourself. I am sure that because of the way you are sitting, you will often experience much pain in your neck and back."

He then carried on to say, that if your fingers become numb after holding out your arms in an outstretched manner, this would indicate a health issue.

"I can see your body, that's why I know your body. Other people didn't want to stop for a while and look at you or give you the attention you deserve but if they did, it would make you feel better." He finished.

Sasha said nothing, because it wasn't her practice to think about herself and she wasn't used to others noticing her.

The following day, he invited her to go with him to Paris.

"I have to take some documents, so we could go together and spend the night there, then return." He suggested.

Sasha said nothing, because it wasn't her practice to think about herself and she wasn't used to others noticing her.

Sasha was silent when his car stopped at hers. Jo also. It was as if they were in silence forever when Sasha asked him quietly:

"What can you see on the surface of the moon?"

"Craters."

"I can see a small girl in a dress with two ponytails who has a dog on a lead."

"Seriously?"

"Yes, I have not told anybody about it before. From now on, every time you see the moon you will think about this."

They were keeping silence for other countless minutes when he started to talk.

"Somebody was born to live and somebody was born to die. Do you know I taught my sister, Tania, how to play chess when she was six years old? I still have this chessboard. I remember she was fond of horses and I always told her stories while we were learning about the different chess pieces and the game. Horses went to sleep in their stable. The Queen lived in a big castle. I have not enough patience to play chess, but I taught Tania to be patient."

"How?"

"I chose the longest queue in the shop. And I suggested that she pay attention to how the people are standing, what they are doing, how they are paying for their purchases. And then we were reading the information given on the wrapping or packaging. She tried to guess why I bought this item and not another one. She could already speak four languages at the age of twelve. When we were travelling anywhere by car, I taught her to understand the meaning of the details, shown on the vehicle number plate. In order to get her used to being in the car, I drove her for many hours around the country. I taught her how to shoot, how to fish, how to make a fire, how to change the engine oil, how to change the wheel and how to check the brakes on the car. Well, we had good times back then. Now, she is already sixteen and, in a few years', she will become a Doctor.

Out of the blue, Sasha said, "You're the most incredible man in my life."

"I sent her on make-up courses because I wasn't capable of teaching her how to do this. But I remember exactly how she spent all my money using my credit card. I always taught her that she could get what she wants from me if she asked politely, otherwise she would get nothing. No naughtiness, no begging but with smile. One day, I remember she wanted to buy a toy in a shop and behaved poorly until she got what she wanted. I bought her this toy and gave to her on the way home only when she had calmed down. One day I broke a toy and, in another situation, I threw a toy out of the car window. She didn't become naughty after that. Some people think this sort of actions is not the right way to treat a small girl. At some point in time she stopped eating vegetables and I began to cook spaghetti with courgettes for her. I cooked bolognaise with vegetable sauce until the day when she began to eat vegetables again. This sauce. How long did it take me to cook it each time? Four hours... Look! Sasha. The world around is wonderful. It all depends on how you make your world."

The following day, he invited her to go with him to Paris.

"I have to take some documents, so we could go together and spend the night there, then return," he suggested.

Within half a second Sasha replied. "I am ready to go with you even if the destination is a very small, remote village"

Chapter 4

She saw Paris only through the window of his car. Everything was strange. They arrived at the city in the evening at around eight p.m. For some reason, Jo did not choose the hotel that he previously has used, and Sasha felt that he was getting more and more nervous every minute, the nearer they got to their destination, he stopped talking to her, and gripped the steering wheel tighter.

She caught his mood, pulling her hair nervously, and also fell silent. Instead he chose one of the hundreds of smaller but unremarkable hotels, although he had asked her to bring her passport, they are not required to be checked here. They enjoyed their night together, but Sasha couldn't help thinking that something was bothering him. At some time after midnight, Jo went out to get a breath of fresh air and when he returned, fifteen minutes later, he seemed nervous and worried.

Sasha hadn't imagined that their first night together would be like this, so she hid her feelings. It had destroyed all of her dreams for one night. In actual fact, she did not see anything of Paris that day.

Sasha was almost thirty-five, the age at which you realise the implications of some of the actions that you could, or do take, whereas at the age of twenty, you rush into adventures without thinking about the consequences. At the age of thirty-five, you realise that a flirtation could be a romantic illusion, and often have already had a bad relationship experience, resulting in your trust in people having been destroyed.

This wasn't the situation here with Jo, she wanted to love him, and be loved in return by him, but this would mean she would have to overlook some of her concerns that seemed to have arisen.

During the night when he left her for a while, he was constantly making telephone calls, and when he returned, she could not determine what he was thinking, or what his mood was, which really hurt her.

The heartache revealed itself, in different ways at different times, sometimes it was as if she was being violently strangled and was barely able to breathe, other times she felt as though her heart had been ripped out of her chest, with then the resulting injury causing yet more pain, or, it felt as though she was being stabbed repeatedly in the heart.

All of these events resulted in much unhappiness, and although the passing of time allowed healing to occur, deep scars remained in place. There were many scars and before each one had fully healed, another appeared. Throughout her life she had suffered in these ways. What caused this pain? She knew the answer.

We are all responsible for our actions and she realised this on her way to Paris. Her castle built of sand, hope and thoughts crumbled, she got what she wanted and even more, would she repeat this experience again? Yes. She always chose emotions in any of their forms, they gave the ability to breathe out fully which brought her alive.

At thirty-five years old, you can get up from your knees, shake yourself off and carry on going. You already know that no matter how many days you moan or complain about wounded feelings, nothing will change. Just try to find pluses and go forward. You cannot stand still, if you do, it will kill you faster.

She needed time, maybe a couple of days to forget, and she wasn't ready to allow her thoughts to meet her feelings. The human brain is capable of forgetting everything quickly, not completely, of course. Our conscious part sends everything that hurts us into the unconscious part, one picture changes to another. Perhaps in a couple of days she will only remember the citizen of Paris leaving his residence, whom she noticed when near the entrance to the hotel.

He had mop curly blond hair and was carrying a young girl that looked around five years old, who was dressed in a typical parisienne coat. She wondered if she was his daughter. He probably took her to the kindergarten, or maybe they were going to visit her granny who lived in one of the suburbs. Who knows? Everybody has their own life story and responsible for their deeds.

Each person, generally speaking can choose the direction in which to travel and must be able to handle any repercussions arising from his or her actions.

Sasha accepted the consequences of her actions completely, and moved on, but she already knew that she would not be able to forget.

For, four hours that morning, they were driving in complete silence, even during the break there was no talking. Only on one occasion did he ask whether everything was okay, and that was just to be polite. Sasha was also silent. And did not know whether she could find the right words which wouldn't sound silly or tactless at that time.

On their way back, Jo pulled into a gas station, he then called somebody on the telephone, she heard him argue with the caller loudly about something then came back to the car, he felt as if he was a stranger, Sasha just looked out of the car window and pretended she wasn't interested in his behaviour.

When their journey had come to an end and he had stopped the car outside of her place she opened the door and got out, as she was about to close the door he said. "I will call you later"

As she made it inside and looked at her phone, she noticed that he had blocked her from having any more communication with him, instantly she felt sad and hurt, but still she couldn't stop thinking about him.

It's been two days since she has returned from Paris and for those two days Sasha has not been able to control her emotions, her tears have been flowing like a burst damn, not only has she been crying over the recently event, but of all the pent-up feelings of the past four years, she sits looking out of the window watching the cars pass by as she sips on her coffee.

On her first day back in St Petersburg, she postponed all of her appointments, and instead decided to go for a run, she hated this activity, at one time, and even at school, she either hardly ran, or was very bad at it, but now, she was happy to run, as whilst running, her thoughts and pain were left behind, as couldn't keep up with her.

Each day she was running further and further, and neither snow, rain, or strong icy cold winds could stop her. After a few minutes of running, her hands became cold, and her brain then seemed to think about this, which gave relief from the other things that were worrying her.

At night Sasha has the same dream. She sees herself in a theatre, and cannot understand why she is there, and she is with her psychoanalyst.

But, two years ago, she was busy with a British project working twelve hours a day. On a monthly basis, she had this Jewish psychoanalyst, who lived in London. He convinced her that despite her arduous working hours, she was happy. He was interested in whether her chair was comfortable, the brand of coffee she drank and whether the coffee was good for her. On each of his visits to Russia, he took her to the theatre, and they held numerous conversations together.

On this night, her dream was that she was in the theatre with him again.

"People were still entering into a small dimly lit room when suddenly, actors appeared on the stage, and then it seemed that the actors had already begun to perform without noticing that people were still entering the hall and looking for their seats, the hall lighting had not been completely switched off.

Her psychoanalyst sat on the right side on the first row concentrating on the acting, and she was sitting near to the back of the theatre behind him, he paid no attention to her. Sasha was trying to understand what the actors were saying, and at this moment, a young handsome man with blond hair, looking at her hand said.

"You have beautiful long fingers."

It is not true, Sasha thought.

Really, her fingers were of normal length.

"You have got an amazing ring with a stone, which kind of stone is it?" he asked.

"This is a stone of love." She answered.

Sasha wore this ring with its big Larimar stone having bought it many years ago in the Dominican Republic. Local people say that this stone can only be found on this island and that it helps anybody who wears this stone to find love. Bright blue with thin remarkable white steaks, a little similar to turquoise.

"Do you have love in your life?" he asked.

Sasha did not answer. After a few minutes, this strange young man took her hand and started to talk about something, *probably, he was talking about his life*, Sasha thought.

She squinted, but with the lack of light in the hall, she was unable to see him clearly, but she noticed he had, blond wavy hair, and pupils the colour of blue water. Almost without blinking he looked into her eyes, spoke very quietly and she had to make an effort to hear what he was saying. And he spoke so slowly and repeatedly paused between words as if he wanted to emphasise each word.

Sasha looked for her psychoanalyst, but his interest was on the stage, and he didn't turn around. Noise from people entering the room and moving between rows annoyed Sasha more and more. It wasn't easy for her to concentrate. She looked at this young man again. He continued to talk to her.

"I was waiting for you, only for you. I cannot live without you anymore. You feel the same. You are my other half. Now, your life go in another direction."

"At some point, Sasha began to feel that she could trust his words. She was sitting in this strange place, looking into his marble eyes and began to believe in everything he said.

She was ready to follow this stranger to where ever he wanted to take her, but then she noticed that there was nobody on the stage, and that the actors were joining and sitting with the audience. She then realised that the young man talking to her was just an actor, and his words were only part of the performance, she looked at him in confusion. His marble eyes were still looking at her, honestly, and with intent.

He smiled softly and said.

"You are mine, aren't you? That's true."

She looked around and found that her psychoanalyst was still in his seat and staring at an empty stage, it seemed to Sasha that he might be imagining that a performance was happening on the deserted stage and that only he knew what was going on there.

Sasha again concluded that the young man with the marble eyes was just an actor, and at the same time, he realised that she had determined that he also was an actor. But he continued talking about her destiny, which had already joined them. Nothing that is happening around them could change the meaning of his words. Neither her understanding about his lie, nor his understanding that she knows about it.

He goes on talking, because he knows that she is ready to listen to him, ready to accept everything and even ready to be cheated. At this moment, Sasha wants to exit the theatre, but she cannot. Marble eyes unexpectedly became those dark amber eyes of Jo, and they prevent her from leaving. Having seen Jo's eyes in this man she wants to trust what she hears. She has always wanted to believe and trust, but in the past, this trust has led to much pain. Surprisingly, now, amber reverted to marble but had become cruel and very angry. A stranger squeezes her wrist. She feels pain. She's looking at him and notices that he's not interested in her any more. She irritates him because he doesn't like the way she looks at him or smiles at him and because she is not endowed with the fingers he likes, and because she trusts him.

It now becomes apparent that she finds herself in a sandpit. Numerous mountains of sand around her, and there is nobody around, she was sinking into the sand, tried to get out and creep forward but sand ran through her fingers and became lodged under her fingernails. She stopped trying to get out of her predicament and her situation became worse. Sand was already in her mouth, in her eyes and on her body. She cried and shouted, sinking deeper and deeper. It was getting hard to breathe. All she saw around her turned into sand. It was her sand castle and walls of this castle are washed by water of inevitable tears.

Tears are always associated with pure eyes and words of love.

Sasha shouted and woke up.

After a month had passed, Sasha decided to write to Jo using a number he would not recognize. It was her birthday soon, and all she wanted was to see Jo again.

[Text]: Thank you for everything.

She typed it out and pressed send without re reading it, within minutes she saw that he had read it, but did not bother to reply.
A week later and she still hadn't heard anything, so she sent him another one.

[Text]: I will be in Belgium for five days starting next week.

To her surprise he replied within minutes.

[Text] I will be with you for three days in Belgium.

It was the night before the flight and she was so excited she couldn't sleep, the thought of seeing Jo again, were running through her head. She hoped that this meeting would be better than the last.

*

The first day in Belgium and Sasha chose the most alluring dress for the meeting with him, it was a short black sleeveless leather one, it was figure hugging tight, with a zip down the back.

"Do you like my dress," Sasha asked on the way to the restaurant.

"Yes, you look amazing."

"There is a zip down the back, which you unzip in two seconds."

Then he smiled.

"You are teasing me. I am sure I can manage in one second."

Sasha was nervous throughout the day, and it was only when she saw how he was looking at her could she relax. He was talking to her whilst driving, about things of some importance.

He had sold his business and had decided to get a yacht so that he could be free to do what he dreamed of. To sail aimlessly into the sunset.

"You had just left Belgium, and on that day, I had an offer for my business. I agreed to sell, signed the contract which included the condition to not lay off any employees except for those whose work was substandard, remembering that most people cannot produce the best work at all times. In any case, all of them were taken care of. Then I sailed to France, a couple of days in Spain, then Portugal and then Spain again. Later, when on board I received and then read your SMS. But decided to not reply at once. I waited to see whether you would write again, and of course, you did write. I anchored my yacht in the marina, got into the bus and for four hours was accompanied by local pensioners until; I reached the airport en route to our meeting. I have only three days and then I will fly back. I ordered many useful things for my vessel Destiny. I will carry out some small repairs for a week and will then sail to Morocco and stay there for another week. What will follow, I don't know. Probably, I will be on the high seas for one year alone."

He paused and then asked whether you know that when you cut the connection with the world you get such amazing feelings.

"Try this, and you will enjoy."

We are driving to my favourite restaurant where I often have supper here alone. It is located on the bank of a river in an old water pumping station building. You will appreciate it."

On the journey there Sasha was wondering how she could draw closer to him, to kiss him. They last met a month ago, and since then she needed his company so much.

Whilst running in the mornings she was thinking about him, she even found time for lunch, because she knew he wanted her to eat regularly and to drink plenty of water. He said to her that this is important.

The restaurant was brilliant, outside it was grey and unremarkable, whereas inside, it looked like the best restaurant in St Petersburg.

Between the first and the third floor, there were remains of the water pumping station from the last century, in the middle of the hall there was no floor, similar in construction to the yards from which well were sunk in St Petersburg, a fence erected on bulky black containers was in place to prevent people from falling into the well.

They were the first into the dining area and sat at a table for two near to this fence.

Jo looked great he wore a white striped shirt, it was not a boring classic style, but with a piece of denim on the sleeve cuffs, dark blue jeans and dark blue jacket of cotton.

Sasha was in the black leather dress with loose hair, which hung down to just below her waist with high healed, black patent leather, designer shoes.

These shoes, because they were so difficult to walk in, gave her the excuse to hold Jo's hand getting from the car into the restaurant.

At the table, he ordered the best dishes for her that evening, they were drinking wine and talking continuously.

As usual, Sasha noticed nobody except him, but by now the restaurant had filled, and there were no tables available, as impressive old Belgium men occupied all of the tables.

On the long passage between the first and the third floor there was a table at which twenty people were seated, behind it was a company of women all aged about forty in formal dresses with men dressed in dinner suits and black ties.

"Look," says Jo, "These people are all drinking the same kind of white wine, and look, it is funny, there's a guy making a speech, and nobody is looking at him or listening to him, but after finishing speaking, everyone is applauding him."

Sasha is already used to how many little things Jo noticed around him and how many things and people irritated him.

"Do you know that I'm glad we met again, I thought I would never see you again," she said.

"Sasha, sometimes we think we are going in the right direction, but later we discover that we took a wrong turning. Now that we have met again it appears that things will be all right in the end. You are here, me too, and we still have two days together, but my destiny and the sea are waiting for me. Perhaps next year we can meet again, and you will sail with me for two weeks."

Maybe it is just his fantasy Sasha thought. She still had painful memories following his disappearance after last time they were together.

"What do you want for dessert?" he enquired, after the wine had all been consumed.

Sasha looked at the menu and realised straight away that she only recognised one of the items on offer, that was crème brûlée.

"Crème brûlée. Yes, I want that."

"Are you serious? what does it mean, "crème brûlée?" he teased her in a French accent, I guess, he joked, that you only order crème brûlée with salad on all of your dates. This is the kind of food that people who know nothing about cuisine order. crème brûlée isn't cooked here in the restaurant. It is delivered in a package. How can you get to know the range of food that is available to eat if you only order the dishes that are delivered to the restaurant in a package? Then he said.

"Forget about crème brûlée."

He called a waiter and said something in French. She hadn't tried such a tasty desert for a long time.

Pieces of mandarin and chocolate cake in a delicate berry mousse and something else, which gave the berry, mousse a variety of flavours. It was a gorgeous dinner in a gorgeous restaurant.

Afterwards, when they went to the seafront, Sasha awaited a kiss. But it was not given.

They got into the car. Sasha found the little cardboard box that she had left in the car, within which was a small silver compass on a black thread, and she said that this compass will lead you to the life you want and will bring you luck.

"Thank you. You know that I have always wanted to be tattooed with a picture of a compass. Your gift is worth wearing and I will put it on later."

Sasha thought with sadness that he would not wear it, but next morning, she saw that it was on his wrist. Sasha's happiness at seeing Jo wear her gift to him was as great as that she felt when seeing a rainbow and all of its colours at that moment.

Now, he leant over and kissed her at last.

After ten minutes, they disentangled, and she started to breathe again.

She missed his beard rubbing against her cheeks, his skin smell, his fingers on her neck, and his breath which she heard clearly now."

"Let's go. I will take you home, it is already late." He looked intently into her eyes and smiled. He was holding her hand in his. She was happy again, but it was happiness with a little sadness.

He parked his car near an abandoned fence, endless fields and trees, one kilometre from the house, the moon was shining so brightly that the route of a narrow winding road and the outline of trees was visible. If anybody passed nearby, they would see the car and, behind misted up car windows, would see two silhouettes, united as one.

She had never been so excited in the past and laughed when it was over. It was the most crazy and desirable sex in her life. Her dress was on the floor in the car. It had really been unzipped in one second.

The Second Day

His car drew up on the left side not far away from the house as usual and as usual, he did not get out the car. His first words were.

"We will go to Antwerp today instead of our planned trip to the sea, if you don't mind, because I am short of time as I'm going to visit my mum at 8.30 p.m. It takes two hours to get to the sea. You know that I can't really refuse to visit my mum. I won't meet my family in the coming months and my sisters are also coming for dinner.

Mum as a rule cooks as if thirty people were coming to eat, so I don't want to disappoint her."

"No problem, yes, it will be Antwerp," she said, who mentally was counting the number of hours less that they would spend together. She so appreciated the extensive and continuous conversation during their journey. He was clever, very intelligent, astute and seemed to be able to talk about anything, which she hadn't experienced with any guy in the past. For instance, he said, it is very harmful to eat Nutella because one of the constituents is palm oil. Roads in Belgium were not designed for so many trucks and this is why there are so many traffic jams every day. Sweets like jelly bears are red in colour and this colouring is extracted from a species of beetle. There are many instances where information of this sort is of no interest or generally not known about by people. He also talked about his yacht.

"Last month, I met an old man in the port who lived with his big shaggy dog of unknown breed, but otherwise alone, on his yacht. I invited him for supper and whilst dining he told me his story. His wife and daughter died in an accident five years ago after which he sold his house and bought a yacht and a dog. He sailed around the world for fifteen years, entering and staying in each bay for only one night, dreaming that one-day the sea will take him forever. A sad story. He could not accept the loss that he had suffered and could not find a home anywhere. The sea became his home. He spent much time fishing and if he was lucky, he sold his catch in each port he visited. I remember his eyes full of much pain even though fifteen years had passed. We drank a bottle of wine during which he recounted other stories about some of the amazing bays he visited. Next morning when I awoke, I found that he already sailed away. One night in each new place. We can be free only inside ourselves; everybody talks about freedom, but nobody can truly feel this. We are all chained to our surroundings, a situation we can't change. I hope the old man finds peace for himself with his dog far from civilisation.

For a couple of minutes, he stopped talking as they were approaching Antwerp. The city was even better than she had imagined, maybe because he had said that it was his favourite Belgium city. Compared to Brussels, there were many larger open spaces, the streets were wider, there were lots of small restaurants on the squares only a few steps from each other, a noisy street with pedestrians and shops selling cheap products, most of which seemed common to other European cities. But Sasha definitely likes this city. They went to the seafront and Jo explained the uses to which these four-hundred-year old buildings were put, their history and everything about them. For one second, Sasha became ashamed of the fact that although she had lived in St Petersburg for twenty years, she knew much about her city but not so much that he knew about Antwerp. They were lucky with the weather.

The sky was blue, the sun shone, there was a light breeze, it wasn't so hot and though they walked holding each other's hands tightly, for half an hour they were sweat free. The best weather, the best city in Belgium, the best man with me, Sasha thought to herself, again looking around at the beautiful building made of brown brick with the high spire.

During the walk she was wondering how she could take a photo of him, but he wasn't interested in posing with a lovely smile or it seemed having his photograph taken at all. Later, when Sasha was taking some video photos, he went behind the camera to avoid being photographed by her. So she sighed and accepted the idea that he would only reside in her memory but not in the phone's gallery. Like other emotional girls, Sasha kept photos of her when taken together with her ex guys in the picture. Rings were given to her in the past and some gifts reminded her of one or other of the ex-men in her past life. She kept but never re-visited except for the times when she needed to recall times that seemed to make her happy. However, it was her illusionary world. Subconsciously she never looked at her past because she knew that she was never happy, And now only Jo in her memory. Sasha thought that he, Jo, was different from other guys and doesn't need to be seen in her photo gallery to be remembered.

Now they are at the seafront, with the water and sea breeze, which they both loved. They weren't looking at the scene before them but can imagine looking over the horizon in the hope of catching the mood of an aimless flight to nowhere. Perhaps real happiness arises from your inner self when you can afford to fly off to anywhere without any particular aim in mind.

There were no people on the seafront at all. They walked onto the bridge and lingered there for a few minutes admiring the views of the river and ships moored nearby.

Jo said that if he wanted to buy a flat in Antwerp one day it would be here.

"Look at the amazing view," he said, pointing at the colourful perfectly clean 20th century constructed buildings with panoramic views available from their attic windows.

"Apartments here cost about forty million. But is it worth it? It is a pity that I don't like Belgium."

Without understanding whether or not she meant it, Sasha said quietly that she didn't like Belgium either.

After such a quick sightseeing walk and learning much about the city he offered to go for a snack. As usual, like on other days, as he seemed interested in her likes and dislikes, he first questioned what she'd like to eat. It seemed strange to her that he asked her this, because in the past guys hadn't. Their selfish habit was to go to the restaurant or cafe they liked, even at the beginning of the relationship, to surprise and impress her with high prices and luxury, whereas Sasha would choose a simple pasta 'Bolognaise' found in a cosy Italian cafe.

For the first couple of minutes, the question confused her. In fact, she did not know what to order.

"What about you? What would you like to eat?" Sasha was trying to find an easy way out of answering his question.

"It doesn't matter for me Sasha. It is important to me that I order for you, what you want."

"Pasta. I like Italian cuisine."

"I know a perfect Italian restaurant near the fifty-year-old cathedral. Give me your hand and let's go."

Now they are sitting at the table facing each other and she eating her favourite pasta. He was eating meat with a spaghetti bolognaise. For aperitif, he ordered a Martini, 'as he guessed that this is what she wanted. Having finished his main course he began to tell her about the framed photo that hangs in his room.

"Bright eyes of a young Bedouin in dark blue clothes, this photo was taken by a photographer from the National Geographic magazine. It is a Bedouin of the Tuareg tribe. They are referred to as dark blue people because of their skin colour. They wear dark blue coloured clothes in which they are completely enclosed and only their eyes are visible. In the desert, they don't colour their clothes in the usual way but instead, blue dye is driven into the fabric with a stone. The Tuareg tribes wear this sort of clothing for the whole of their life. As years pass, their clothes loose colour because of the sun but dye penetrates the skin which over time acquires an indelible bright blue shade. In the past, the Tuareg tribe scattered across different African countries. The pain of this forced separation is still transmitted in the stories told by mothers to their children. Pain cause by absence of their homeland and oppression by other nations is still heard during night conversations near the bonfire. Look carefully at the photo. In the pupils of the eyes of this young Tuareg you can see the reflection of a gun barrel directed at him. But there is no suspicion of fear in his expression. It looks as though he is ready to face any challenging eventuality. His eyes burn with a thirst for life, and that's how you must live. I take this photo with me and hang in my new home wherever that is. It is the only thing to which I am attached."

Sasha thought about this story for a long time and imagined herself as being him, this young Bedouin from the desert, with no fears and so much will to live.

After she had returned home, she ordered a copy of this same photo, to be mounted in a thin black frame, which, when received will be in her house wherever that may be.

After lunch was finished, Jo asked Sasha whether she would like another drink. Without hesitation she blurted out "Aperol", then remembering after a second that it was Jo's most hated liquid.

"What? This is muck! Order plutonium, it is better poison. It has at least a bright green colour instead of a chemical orange. How can you drink this at all, it's not even a cocktail? They mix one bad substance in an unnatural coloured liquid made of beetles with another one. If you want a real cocktail, order a normal one."

Sasha said, smiling, "You are so nice. I was just waiting for your lecture about 'Aperol'."

"No, wait, I'm not like your old boy friends who weren't interested in what you drank. Has nobody ever told that this is shear muck?"

"No," Sasha started to laugh.

"Aperol," Jo continued, "do you know how it is made? although you don't need this information. I can see you 'really love yourself', so just drink anything you want. Oh my God. I get irritated even if I look at this drink."

He called over a waiter and said something to him in Dutch.

"Orange chemical liquid, bravo Sasha, a perfect choice. Yesterday it was crème brûlée from the packet. Today it is this."

He threw back his head, looked closely at Sasha, then shook his head.

"You know that if I don't like it, I won't pay."

In a second, a big glass of 'Aperol', a spirit glass containing one small measure of a clear liquid and a plate with pieces of cheese were brought to the table.

"You know that lunch must not be finished with a dessert, but with cheese, otherwise you will get a heavy feeling which is not what you need in the afternoon. First, I will try and if it is what I want you will try," he said, using a toothpick to pick up some blue cheese. He kept it in his mouth for a while and drank some clear liquid similar to vodka.

"Fine, now you will try. Take a piece of cheese and keep it in your mouth for a while, let it melt and then drink a little "grappa". Wait, only a little, otherwise you will spoil the taste. Keep it for a little while in your mouth. And now, don't forget to stir your nice "Aperol"."

Then he took hold of the straw in her glass and stirred the cocktail himself.

"Look, the most delicious of the cocktail is at the bottom of the glass. Enjoy."

At this moment, Sasha didn't want to drink the cocktail at all. She had already tasted so many shades of flavour, so it seemed to her it was a bad idea to order "Aperol," but for appearances sake, and because of stubbornness, she stirred it again and drank a little. The taste seemed awful. How was it possible that in the past she had drunk this concoction so many times? Perhaps as a result of being with the wrong men, with men who were not interested in what she drank or ate or her feelings.

"Maybe you want a photo with "Aperol"? It will warm you up on the cold nights in St Petersburg."

At that moment, photos of her during her Rome visit with "Aperol" flashed past her eyes, the first and the second time always with the wrong men in her life. She blushed inwardly but could not offer a reply.

"Okay, I stop to joke about "Aperol", but if you continue to drink it, I will look the other way. And what about "grappa"? Do you want me to order it for you?"

"Yes, I want you to order it, it's very tasty."

They departed the restaurant and the "Aperol" remained untouched on the table.

Third day

When they had returned to the village in the middle of nowhere, as Jo like to joke, she wrote him a message saying,

[Text]: Tomorrow only you and me, I want to be completely alone with you.

He replied.

[Text]: You want me? I ordered a sauna for the morning.

The sauna was a detached building located on the premises of typical private Belgium house. It was clean and nice inside. A jacuzzi with a ceiling through which stars could be seen, A swimming pool from which a view of the sea is possible. Two saunas and upstairs a big sofa on the glass floor. They were alone, not dressed and there were no towels.

Naked bodies in warm soft water, naked bodies on the sofa under the roof with the transparent ceiling, and no stars visible that night. But don't you need them at this moment? They absorbed each other's bodies as much as possible, each motion coinciding with her thoughts and desires.

Already, the first kiss had sent signals to her brain which had cause a sensation similar to an electrical discharge taking place throughout the body. The permissive nature of their entanglement brought about pleasurable feelings in every square millimetre of their bodies. And if yesterday everything was likened to a hurricane, today he wasn't in a hurry, he took his time, unbearable amounts of fluids flowed, and penetration was really deep.

How many sensational emotions can a body withstand in a minute?

Especially if these minutes are of infinite length. Everything normally important to her became irrelevant at this time, her only concentrated interest was his smell, his clouded amber appearance, the power of his fingers squeezing and caressing her neck, her hips, her waist and her breasts. She belonged only to him at this time and these were the best moments of her life.

After that, they were silent, she laying close to him inhaling his smell. If only you could carry him home on your back, she thought. He was looking at her and smiling.

"It was a good idea to rent that sauna," he joked, ending the silence.

Sasha smiled, "As are all your ideas," she said.

Thirty minutes remained before they had to part, so Sasha was desperate to gaze at him without a break and tried to recall each minute of that day. She knew that he didn't like to kiss and hug much and he didn't normally want to hold her hand in the car, but he would squeeze her hip and pat her thigh. He always needed his own space. Sasha wanted to learn how to be confident without a man. Not to lose herself in a useless relationship and it the most difficult thing for her. All she got from past guys, before Jo, devastated her and left her with nothing. They used her weakness and were desperate for her to become addicted to them, and then later they resumed their own selfish lifestyle.

For a long time, she felt as if she was a small dog being dragged along on the end of a lead. Jo was completely different, he taught her to look after herself, to love herself, to value herself, and her life in any relationship.

"Will you miss me tomorrow?" he asked her whilst sitting in the jacuzzi.

"You know the answer."

"Yes, but tell me."

"Yes, I will."

"And as for me, I will be okay." He smiled.

"Do you think it would be important to me if you do not write to me in a couple of days?"

"No, sure not. This is not important."
Again, he smiled.
"Your birthday will be soon, the 23rd?"
Intentionally he messed up the date, it was a joke. In the water Sasha kicked him lightly.

"Look, you must live as if you have a birthday every day, celebrate each day, sing 'happy birthday' every morning, is not the date of birth so important? my birthday is on the 1st of November which is the day of remembrance for relatives who have passed away."

People visit the cemetery on this day, and Jo celebrates his birthday.

"Tu-Tu," he indicated with his outstretched arm as if a train driver.

"We have what we have, if you want to get more from your life, just go forward, there is no sense in waiting for, or demanding it, even if we just drank coffee together I would be happy, even if you didn't have one-half of what you have and worked in the cosmetic shop as a sales assistant, I would be with you here and now. Even if you had two wives and five children, I would be with you, here and now." Sasha said, "it doesn't matter who you are, or what you are, you give me emotions and inspire me, and that is important."

He kissed her on the cheek.
"We have to leave, let's go."

After hearing these words, it was as if a crack had appeared in the day, getting wider as time approached for their parting.

Sasha felt that one side of the crack belonged to the time they spent together, and the other side without him.

"Kiss me," Sasha said, as she hugged him on his neck.

He kissed her, only briefly, though she wanted more.

"Now, I will smell like a brewery, how can I drive?" He joked.

Sasha smiled with sadness.

What else could she do it was not easy to be humoured at that moment.

They exited the sauna; Sasha shook her wet hair and took a deep breath because she felt that soon there would not be enough air.

On the way back, they were not talking about anything important, and nothing was said about any future meeting.

After parking outside the house, Jo said.

"I will write to you later."

"Last time you said exactly the same," she replied.

"Last time you got out of the car and didn't even look back."

"Say, have a good day."

"Have a good day."

"No, that's not exactly what I want, just kiss me and I will go."

Jo drew Sasha closer and gave her several quick kisses.

"Okay, I'm leaving," she said, subconsciously trying to stay with him for a couple of extra minutes.

She stayed for a couple more seconds, kissed him quickly and jumped out of the car.

He pressed the accelerator and drove off.

In her mind's eye, he disappeared after a few moments. She seemed to freeze at the house entrance and these few seconds felt like unbearably long minutes, when his car disappeared round the bend it became so difficult to breathe.

Instead of going indoors, Sasha turned around and went for a walk along a narrow ash felted road in the middle of a forest and fields in this Belgium back woods, there were no sounds but in her mind she heard furious animal screams of her heart, then she felt, as if this pain might explode like an atomic bomb and in an instant, all of these irritating green flat fields of grass, red brick houses so similar to each other, the blue sky with very rare bright white clouds above her head would disappear.

But nothing happened except that her throat tightened, and it became harder to breathe, to get better, people say that you should shout or cry, only, she could not cry, her tears flowed slowly down her cheeks, without distracting from her thoughts, it was the end of the third day.

Now, Jo's company was no longer hers to enjoy.

*

A couple of months later Sasha went to see her psychotherapist. He was strange and perhaps, for the first time in her life, it was this that caused her to go to his second and next sessions. During the initial visit, he was silent for one hour just listening to Sasha and then threw in a phrase, as if by chance, "It's useless to tell the disease what it's called. Think, desire to hold and desire to enjoy. These two desires, if taken together, destroy each other."

He asked Sasha to return the next day. That morning she went upstairs to the clinic second floor. Again, Sasha tried to avoid these thoughts about Jo. Only one question reverberated in her mind. *'When will Jo appear again?'*

The premises was located in the countryside, built in the style of London residences and was enclosed by an high forged metal fence. The building embraced a hospital, where inpatients were treated, room space for group psychotherapy sessions, rooms for sensory relaxation, plus management staff office space. Sasha chose the most senior doctor from the clinic for her sessions. To make an appointment with this doctor was incredibly difficult even if you had connections in the psychoanalyst world. Sasha was lucky that due to a cancellation by another patient, she was able to get an appointment for two days hence. She arrived at the session room, grasped the ornate door handle, threw back her long hair and without knocking, quickly entered to room. Almost everything was white! The wall was lined with white leather, the short-pile carpet was white, there were white lilies on a white lacquered table on which there were white papers arranged in order, a patient case note file which was white, and a thin white notebook. The sense of cleanliness was only marred by a huge bright red leather armchair which belonged to the owner of the room. It was impossible to take your eyes off this bright coloured object whilst in this white 'paradise'. *Perhaps most patients think about the mistakes in their lives and criminals about their wrong doings,* Sasha thought for a moment, but suddenly, a loud voice said, "Alexandra, you are seven minutes late today. We are OK?"

It was his favourite phrase — used several times a day when addressing staff and patients. The voice belonged to an old man. He had nice blond hair, curled at the ends, that reminded Sasha of a small curly haired boy whose hair his mother forgot to cut. For sure because of greyness it wasn't possible to see him as a small boy.

If you could see this old gentleman's hands you would realise that he was under sixty. Nothing suggested his real age except his hands. He has the back of a thirty-five-year-old guy because he trained his muscles every day. His face, with minimal wrinkles, indicated an age of forty-five. Eyes. Eyes did not reveal any information. Light blue, very clear, as if they were from mountain spring water. Time left no sign of any turbidity. Only a slight smile from the corner of the lips similar to that seen in the portrait of Mona Lisa by Leonardo da Vinci gave any information that might have arisen from past problems in his life about his experience and cunning. The voice of a doctor depended on with whom he was talking. For instance, with his patients, he was like a 'huge lazy boa' who hadn't yet decided whether to squeeze the person's neck or to give the opportunity to breathe for a while.

With colleges he didn't employ this form of strangulation but instead, made it clear to them with his professional smile, that he always invisibly close to them, and wouldn't tolerate any gossip behind his back or any disobedience. Sasha never saw the doctor with friends so she suspected he had none. Sometimes he made session appointments for Friday evenings and Sasha thought 'It meant that nobody was waiting for him at home, like me'.

The doctor communicated exclusively in sign language with his staff and over many years of service in this job everyone has learnt to understand him. Sometimes during communication, he whispered and was confident that everybody present in the large room would hear him. He enjoyed listening to his patients for hours on end. He waited and demanded replies only from them. The doctor claimed that the best rehabilitation would occur at his Russian clinic. He emphasised that he could provide physical as well as psychological support there. Any patient who visited this doctor finally revealed secrets of their lives. Patients used to call him 'Sargun' (a God). But in fact, he was professor Nicholas Sargunof. Nicholas had his favourites among the patients. There was a group who accepted him not only as a doctor, but as a coach. Another group of patients remained aloof and were doomed to loneliness. They had their own special room-based dining schedule, special short distance walking schedules, and no books except for existentialist writers Sartre and Camu. These patients had no connection with the outside world. Several months later they were ready 'to talk to a plate of soup' and suddenly 'Sargun' appeared. Just like a snake, he silently slithered into their ward, circled and then slowly coiled himself around them. And as a result of this, patients burst into tears and then talked about their childhood, misunderstanding parents, about the toy car they hadn't received on their fifth birthday, their father's lovers, about their first unrequited love and etc. Soon they began to feel comfortable in the coil into which the doctor had encircled them. Sargun loved such patients like children loved to eat frozen homemade ice cream. Several times, on passing his office, Sasha heard him shouting very loudly at somebody. One day, following an invitation, she entered his cabinet, noticed huge pieces of a broken porcelain vase laying on the snow-white coloured plush carpet, a broken pencil on the table and a large area of fat stain on one of his shirt sleeves. Sargun didn't bother to explain what had happened. On two occasions Sacha noticed dandruff remains on this old man's snow-white coloured medical gown and dirt under flawlessly polished nails of his aristocratic fingers. All of this confused her. Very often, standing outside of his room, awaiting entry, she would try to predict the 'weather' on the other side of the door. From time to time, during their session, he was silent, occasionally nodding his head. Sometimes, Sasha couldn't reply to any of his questions and realised she liked to tell him about Jo. Sargun almost never interrupted her.

She could talk about Jo for an hour continuously. It seemed that the doctor didn't tire of listening to her. Sasha returned again and again to the snow-white coloured cabinet.

That day, Sargun did not give her the opportunity to pour out details of her suffering because he interrupted in the middle of the sentence, smiled, and then started to speak slowly. 'The emergence of a new feeling occurs in each person differently. You can make comparisons with disease. Some people have rather strong immunity and their bodies fight the virus and, on most occasions, with success. Immunity from love can be secured in the same way as immunity from a virus, by vaccination. After that, the body becomes less susceptible to the disease. These days I believe most people have immunity from love. Who needs such love if it causes weakness? Love is the most powerful weapon. Love which forces you to sacrifice life for another person, your lover. Love which could change your settled life in seconds rather like the wind. Love that hammers at your head as though struck with the blunt side of an axe and at that moment everything ceases to exist'.

'And if love cannot be controlled, ideally you could try and build a society in which the public consciousness would accept no place for love. Love would be considered as being of no use, senseless, a useless waste of time. The only ideal — common sense. 'Love makes no more sense than snow in the desert'. With each passing year, more and more people are born without the ability to love. As if deprived of the organ responsible for this feeling. Rationalism came to replace love.

My dear Sasha, "Are you capable of loving?"

"Yes, yes."

"You know Alexandra, I have always loved strong women. I think it not fair for such women to be with weak men. Of course, it would be easier for a strong man to be with a weak woman. It is not fair but it is fact. If I decided to have breakfast every morning with a woman, for sure she would have a modest character, dark hair, with big eyes, with a great belief in everlasting love and victory over evil. But I know, that actually, evil is more powerful than goodness and we don't live in a fairy tale. The energy of evil is much stronger than the energy of goodness. An evil man is always more forceful than a kind man. There are stories with a good ending, but as a rule, evil is the winner. People try not to think about it.

Everybody knows how difficult it is to descend from heaven to earth, and to destroy your sandcastle of hopes and illusions with the sudden appearance of common sense. But time passes and again we start to build illusory houses of sand. We start from the porch because the porch isn't a house yet, then terrace, living room, kitchen and finally the ground floor is ready. Once the ground floor is ready, then the first floor and after that the whole house is completed, beautiful outside but rotten inside. How could you see your house with Jo?"

Part Two

Chapter 1

A young woman in a black dress wearing a black scarf was holding the hand of a ten-year-old boy with big amber eyes. Everyone could see that she was in a hurry. Sometimes she pulled her young son along, passing through the narrow streets of Brussels.

They were desperate to return home from the cemetery having just buried her husband, father of her three children.

Two young sisters, of age two and three years respectively, were being looked after by her woman neighbour because they were too young to watch how their beloved father was lowered into the ground and covered with soil, the mother of the children was either in a hurry to get away from the pain of the burial, or maybe because her child minder neighbour didn't want to care for the sisters for any longer.

There were no tears from the eyes of the boy with the really bright amber pupils, when he felt that the tears might begin to flow, he bit his hand so hard that he hurt himself, but he could withstand this.

At this time, he did not realise yet that his life would change, his father was an ordinary Belgium man who worked as a manager in a small business company.

His father had met his mother, a woman of Muslim faith, in the cafe, and since holding her hand from then had never let it go until yesterday.

Now that her husband had died, she could not expect a large pension, and in a couple of months her savings were finished, she went to work and had two jobs.

This small boy had not realised at the time that his childhood had ended abruptly and that his adult life had just begun, it was a life in which he was the only man in the family, a life in which each day he took care of his sisters.

Year after year his mother worked from morning till night, and she rented a small flat for her and her children in the city suburbs, he took his sisters to kindergarten and to school, prepared breakfast, dinner and supper for them, and daily on the way home carrying the youngest sister in his arms, he looked at Belgium boys chasing a ball in the yard.

He was the oldest of the boys in the yard, the strongest and if as a result of being teased there was any fighting, he could easily win. Several times the school psychologist talked to him about fights with these boys. The boy was silent and gazed intently into the eyes of the doctor, causing him to become nervous, to the extent that he started to fiddle around with his spectacles.

The session finished, and one day the boy said to him, "You just don't want to help me."

The psychologist threw his spectacles on to the table and the boy was no longer asked to see him after that event. The family decided not to send the boy to the university, and he had to earn money from work, so that he could save to use later for study by his younger sister.

He acted as though he was the father to his sisters, and he knew that the reason that his mother was late home on one day a week was that she went to the cafe where she had met his father and sat there until her mint tea was cold.

At the age of sixteen, every day after work, instead of meeting friends, he went to his sister's school to take them home.

He had something that attracted women, he realised that all of the mothers while waiting for their children were looking at him with some interest, one of the mothers of his sister's classmates who was desperately attracted to the bodies of young guys, put her hand on his shoulder and invited him to her home.

In order to avoid meeting, and waiting with these mothers, he arrived to collect his sisters immediately after their classes were over, he mastered several professions by self-education, and he could speak six languages with ease. He promised himself that he would make his mum happy and buy her a house so that she could be the complete hostess, he also promised that he would support his younger sister in her studies to become a doctor and all of his money was used for this. He used the last of his savings to help his older sister if she asked for help.

He is used to working long hours and slept little.

He awoke today at before sunrise, having had the same nightmare.

He again saw the burial of his father, and saw his pale face as he heard his voice saying.

You are my super Jo, and I'm proud of you my boy.

Chapter Two

Jo woke up again this morning at five o'clock, he got up slowly from his bed, and put on his bracelets, there were four, two of them with blue stones, one with a silver chain and the other, his favourite, made with a yacht rope.

This rope reminded him about freedom, and the kind of life he wanted to live.

The young girl, lying beside him in the bed, looked like a nineteen-year old, she had dark hair, long black eye lashes, and was sleeping in a white silk lace top in which she was dressed on their first marriage night one year ago. Jo put on his tea shirt and quietly went to the corridor, he needed to feed a cat, this cat called Luna, a wild cat taken in from the street some years ago.

She ate whatever was offered to her and was like a devoted friend who was always waiting for him when he returned from work, in order to jump up on to his knee, compared to others who lived in this house, he did not have to talk to her.

He tried not to be noisy when passing two rooms on the second floor near the stairs. The times of the day when everybody was still asleep were valued by him, so it didn't matter that he, again, had woken up at five in the morning.

There was a kitchen on the first floor, and it is in this place that he spends most of his spare time, he loves to cook, as in his childhood he had to cook for the family while his mother was working, and he could turn this occupation into an amazing game.

He chose food very carefully, and he knew how to cook the various cuts of meat from the cow, in the upper cabinet there were containers of spices arranged in alphabetical order.

Everything had to be organised in his life so that he could exercise control.

In a narrow hall opposite the kitchen, he looked at his facial expression in the mirror, to check that there was no evidence on his face that he hadn't slept for years, sometimes, during the night he went to the living room to sleep on a narrow uncomfortable sofa there.

He liked to sleep alone, and, liked to be alone. In this life he had too many responsibilities all of which related to his family. He dreamed that one day he would buy a big house on the coast for his family, which would enable him to take his mum away from the place that for twenty years had reminded her of his father.

Jo put some water in his glass and unexpectedly smiled to himself having remembered yesterday's meeting with this strange Russian girl who did not care about her health at all, did not drink enough water, and was eating muck like hamburgers, fried potato with mayonnaise, and chips.

Something in this girl had caused him to smile. Perhaps it was her efforts to seem to be strong, or maybe it was the simple things that surprised her just as if they would a naive child.

For him, she was not a typical Russian woman, Russian people with whom he had had previous contact, liked to display their wealth to everybody, and wore clothes only of famous brands where the label could be easily seen. They were hospitable only because they wanted to show to people the extent to which they had money. Russian girls can always be identified because they wore high heels, used bright lipstick, had plump lips (as a result of some surgical procedure), unnaturally long hair extensions and eyelashes. Everything about their appearance was excessive, but Sasha was completely different. Absence of make-up, her natural long chestnut hair, with barely noticeable copper coloured strands only visible in the sunshine and big hazel eyes. He looked at her eyes yesterday and saw much pain.

You cannot ignore this expression without raising certain questions, and these questions need answering. He was thinking about Sasha that morning and compared to other people he was really interested in her. Jo prepared breakfast, omelette with bacon, added soft cheese and some spring greenery. Now he was ready to go to work. He preferred to travel to the office by train, forty minutes each morning.

Suburbs of Brussels were similar to one large village, where buildings were interspersed with fields on which sheep were grazing and horses walking around. During the journey in the train he could see seventy-eight similar houses, thirty-four stables and twelve pubs.

Jo loved to count things that surrounded him, especially those that caused irritation. In each cafe he could name ten things that irritated him. He noticed all of the small things around him, dried beer stains on the bar counter, dust on the lamp above the table, a small hole on the table covering, two open bottles of one sort of wine and there were many various other details that were of importance to him.

Today in the train he wasn't counting the houses but was writing to Sasha. Jo thought, *she's unlike other people but I had to choose another one.*

The train arrived at the station thirty minutes later.

Chapter 3

When Jo was fifteen years old, he was taught by a young forty-year-old male tutor from Lebanon who had lost both feet from a grenade explosion. This man had been sent to Brussels to select new, and to tutor a new generation of people who could contribute to the war effort. He noticed that Jo's calm and silent manner looked as though he could be a future perspective mercenary. But Mohamed made only one mistake. When fighting with other guys Jo was not cruel enough. He could not kill a person, even if he considered all people as 'rubbish'. Jo lost his father and at that time could not afford to study. Mohamed immediately focused on Jo's weak points. He promised Jo a good education, never mind that it was not at university, and would teach him several languages. He promised Jo that he would be completely able to financially support his mum and sisters. In return he was to carry out some tasks for his 'brothers'. Jo did not accept these people to be his 'brothers' but his thirst for knowledge and the desire to support his family was so great that he accepted the offer.

There we not too many instructions for Jo at this time because Mohammed wanted to keep him in reserve for the more important tasks to be carried out in the future, He wanted to ensure that there were no failures connected with the jobs that any other immigrant from the middle east could easily do. Jo agreed to become a guide. He needed to fly one more time to Syria for a couple of weeks. Mohammed promised a large amount of money for this job so it was worth the risk but before that he has to do one more, simple thing for him.

The previous few months were not successful for Jo, the oldest sister lost her job, the youngest sister needed money to pay for next year's university medical studies, the work contract which had been in place for the last half year had failed before signing, and his mother began to complain about endless headaches.

The previous few months were not successful for Jo, the oldest sister lost her job, the youngest sister needed money to pay for next year's university medical studies, the work contract which had been in place for the last half year had failed before signing, and his mother began to complain about endless headaches.

That morning, he accepted an offer from an acquaintance without thinking, he definitely didn't like people, especially strange Russians.

How is it possible to say that Crimea belongs to them? He really did not understand this.

"Meet her a couple of times, smile and invite her to Paris. Don't forget to check that she takes her passport and telephone. Take her to the hotel. Leave the room and make a call. And then it's our business," said his Muslim acquaintance.

He lived in Europe but could not accept the way of life there, every day he felt envy and ferocious angst which was directed at Europeans.

Jo agreed to do the job.

"The greater the beauty of the woman, the more we will pay."

Jo spent a few days on the site trying to make contact with several girls, but communication did not bring success. Suddenly, he saw her photo, a slim fragile girl, with long brown chestnut hair, arranged in a bun, she was sitting on a windowsill looking out, and her profile indicated that she could fly to Belgium in a week.

That's what he needed, because this meant less additional spending, so money could be saved on tickets, which he could keep for himself.

He wrote her a brief formal message.

She didn't ask unnecessary questions, which was convenient for him. She seemed at first, a little strange to him, with deep thoughts about anything they spoke about. It was difficult to single out any detail, but he viewed her as a whole. She wasn't interested in daily routine and in fact seemed to be living in the clouds.

Chapter 4

Sasha agreed to go to Paris within seconds of the offer being made. *How reckless of her,* Jo thought.

She didn't even ask my surname, and she knows nothing about me, how is it possible to trust me so blindly?

That morning he awoke at five o'clock as usual, he had a different nightmare.

Jo saw Sasha alone in a thin blue silk dress with thin straps. She was standing in the middle of a narrow street, people passing her nearby, and with an endless stream of people in grey clothes with grey empty faces. People started to elbow and hurt her and with more power as time went by. He saw that she was in pain and was looking at him in silence without taking her eyes off him, she cringed from the blows. More and more people gathered around her and now she was in the centre of the crowd. He saw how they had squeezed her and how difficult it was for her to move. She was silent, continued to look at him and her facial expression was one of unbearable pain. Jo woke up abruptly with a distinct feeling of sadness.

He was in the cold shower for a long time trying to recover from the nightmare.

He made coffee and wrote that he would be coming to meet her.

During the journey they spoke to each other a lot, when you drive somewhere, for several hours along the highway, you unconsciously start to talk about things that are difficult to talk about face to face when sitting opposite each other in a café, it is similar to a session with the psychologist.

You are lying on a comfortable sofa, looking at the ceiling, or looking at pictures on the walls, and your companion is a little further away from you, so his eyes can't be seen. That means you cannot fear the reaction from what was said.

Jo talked about the death of his father. Sasha talked about her own life, which at times was quite difficult. Life without concessions and not enough time for rest.

After five hours they were arriving in Paris. Jo checked his phone and noticed an SMS message that hadn't been read, so he opened it.

[Text]: We are waiting in the hotel.

Suddenly, he said,

"Look I have changed my mind we will go to another hotel."

"Okay, it doesn't matter to me." Sasha said.

Chapter 5

He felt free to be with her, though this meant missing many telephone calls, he knew that this was the first, and the last night that they would be together, and because of this, the night became more exciting.

He noticed how her body was moving under his fingers, how her breathing changed, and her pulse rate increased, how she bit her lips again and again when he caressed certain points of her body.

The hotel wasn't remarkable, and it was typical of those found in the region, the room he had reserved, had black walls, no windows, a mirror on the ceiling and floor mounted lighting. Here, you could forget time and relax completely, but while resting, Jo's thoughts were concentrated on the repeated telephone call he had received, and so, could not afford this.

Just after midnight, Jo said.

"Wait for me, Sasha, I will go outside for a breath of fresh air."

She nodded silently.

Jo quickly put on his jeans and T-shirt and went out.

Paris wasn't sleeping, and from the nearby café, voices could be heard of some noisy drunken youths, he was sure that a gang of Africans nearby were looking for a drugs seller.

Jo took his mobile out of his pocket and dialled a number.

"We will not be there. I will return the money to you." Following which, at the other end of the line, men shouting in the Arabic language could be heard, but Jo hung up, and then sent an SMS to his family.

"Don't leave the house without me, I will be home tomorrow."

He wasn't prepared for any of the various possible outcomes arising from the situation in which he now finds himself in, but in any case, he had made his choice. Now, he returned to their room, got into bed under the blanket and cuddled up closely to a sleeping Sasha. Although before he fell asleep, he thought *Sasha will be safe*.

In the morning, whilst drinking coffee, he attempted to sell his motorbike by his phone, and in order to try and hide the fact that he was very nervous, did not look at Sasha.

She was silent, and felt that something was troubling him, but was afraid to ask. But after twenty minutes of silence, she asked quietly.

"Are you in a hurry? Is it possible to drive to the Eiffel Tower on the way back to home?"

Jo very quickly weighed up all of the risks.

"Okay, but just for a few minutes."

They left the hotel holding hands just as they were when arriving yesterday, each having their own thoughts.

Sasha saw Paris through the window of the car. They parked in a small street close to the Eiffel Tower and had only six minutes to admire the view and take two photos. During this period, Jo didn't hold her hand.

With each passing kilometre as they neared 'Sasha's home, stress levels became greater, she remembered that one day, he had said to her, whether she understood when something was worrying him.

"I will be silent," he had said.

And for the present, this was the situation.

When they are near to her home, Sasha had decided that she had gathered sufficient strength to ask him what had happened back at the hotel, but upon looking at him felt that he was not ready to reply. When he stopped the car and politely said.

"I will call you."

A phrase similar to 'how are you' or 'good day'.

Sasha tried to see the expression on his face then nodded, smiled and got out of the car. She went into 'life without Jo' mode, and within twenty seconds, he blocked her number in his phone.

Again, Jo heard inner voices. They became more prominent and more annoying especially when he was alone. Sometimes he could manage this. When in the company of Sasha, these voices were less noticeable. Jo imagined that the voices were directing their attention to Sasha, but after that when he was alone the voices returned to him. They analysed his day, voices interrupted each other and sometimes they called him to the sea. The sea and Sasha were always on his mind. Today he has to fly to this military base again for a one-week trip. And the voices will follow him as usual.

Chapter 6

"How do you want me during our next 'encounter'"?
"I want to be looking into your eyes for the whole time."
"I will close your eyes with my hand."
"If you want to touch me, I will tie your hands together," he said playfully.
"If you want it slowly... I will go faster."
"Why?"
"Because I know more than you do about how you want me to please you."

Jo gazed at Sasha and she in turn could not take her eyes off him, he enjoyed her company very much indeed. Sasha did not notice anybody except for him, but sometimes, because it became noisy, her attention was temporarily distracted.

Frowning, she looked to see where this noise was coming from, and then returned her eyes to look at her guy, Jo.

*

More than a month had passed since their last meeting. They were sitting in his favourite and the most expensive restaurant in Antwerp, which is also, where he took his mother every year on her birthday. At other times, when in this locality, he would sit alone and drink coffee at the table with the seafront view.

He loved solitude, and this was a mutual interest.

Each day spent with Sasha, was straightforward, and at the same time complicated, he was completely at ease with her and had no desire for the company of others. However, he was constantly tormented by the fact that he could not tell her about his real world. She believed that he was a successful businessman with a property portfolio of three houses, who owned a yacht and who enjoyed his life, he knew that the amount of money held in his bank account was of no importance to Sasha, but it did appear to him that she was really worthy of someone of substance and who was wealthy.

Initially, under the then circumstances, he felt it best to not disclose the truth, about some of his activities, he didn't say much at their second meeting because deep down he was so afraid of losing her.

Moreover, he was afraid that the loving looks she gave him would cease. Whenever he came home, the imaginary world in which the possibilities for Sasha with him were endless, abruptly reverted to the reality of the present. He was the ringleader, had responsibilities and wasn't free.

On their last day together this time, the smile on Sasha's face was one of sadness.

"Why are you so sad?" he asked.

"You always know the reply… sometimes it's normal to be sad."

"Sadness has its colour."

"Why?"

"It changes colour dependent on the view."

"I will miss our conversations. It seems to me that I'm looking for something that I cannot find. I try to find any thought hidden in the 'fog' of other unimportant thoughts. And I have the feeling that this thought is close to me but as yet, not found."

"Unhappiness, prefers company."

"Why?"

"When unhappiness and loneliness meet, they create depression and death. Similar things happen with boredom and pain… Like ice and wind. The perfect symbols of suffering."

"But how can I find what I am looking for?"

"Look around. Everything is there surrounding you. That is enough. But did you understand while you were sitting and looking? You have to do this and finally except."

"I will. I have enough time and no need to hurry."

"You know that there are a million reasons to be happy, so pay no attention to the thousand that make you unhappy," Jo said, embracing her.

She was such a fragile person, inside and outside.

"Remember three things, never allow anyone to raise their voice at you, never become unhappy if things that are said to you aren't true and don't allow your heart to cry if the bottle is already empty."

He stopped talking and cuddled her continuously for a couple of minutes.

"And don't forget to go running. Sport is real fun, Well, now let's go to a quiet spot where nobody will disturb us."

Chapter 7

This morning Jo woke up because of a nightmare that brought him his memory. He saw again the Military base. It was his second time there. Jo heard loud shouting. He went out of the tent. The first rays of the sun were visible behind the hills. The day was expected to be unbearably hot and long. Four wounded combatants were brought to the base, two of whom were the very young guys, Jo immediately recognised from last time because he remembered seeing the bright flash of fear in their eyes. And two new older guys. Since his first trip there were almost no familiar faces left in the camp. Jo had a photographic memory and accordingly could describe in detail anyone with whom he had had contact with previously. Sometimes Jo wanted to forget everything and go to the sea forever: 'being free gives rise to happiness'. The distressed shouting of wounded people brought Jo back to reality. A few seconds were enough to realise these two young guys would not survive. They were to be shot if the doctor confirmed that they wouldn't live despite medical care. Jo already knew that these two young people would going to die. As a rule, in this war, fatally wounded personnel were shot dead to prevent the enemy capturing them, but the less severe wounded were taken back to camp. Because some of the fighters had no strong beliefs, but instead were motivated by money, if they were captured and tortured, they would disclose everything they knew to their captors. This group of people were very careful to avoid combat but, in most cases, luck is given to the reckless. That's why the finale is almost always a forgone conclusion.

Wounded people were attended by the local doctor. Jo went back to his room because he knew what would happen later. In a few minutes came the sound of two shots. Jo woke up and memories flashed back as it all happened yesterday. The other two guys who were suffering in silence, were operated on as soon as conditions permitted in this military base. For them torment was goodness. In two weeks, they will be sent to the nearest town to become suicide bombers and will take with them dozens of people who valued their life...

Three days, seventy-two hours, four thousand three hundred and twenty minutes, passed by more quickly than he would have liked, they should say 'goodbye' to each other, but he wasn't capable of doing this.

Early in the morning, he had to take a bus to Spain, and for nearly twenty-four hours, he would be travelling in a dirty dusty vehicle within which there would be twenty things around, that irritated him, though in itself, this wasn't particularly important. It won't be too long now before he was busy with the yacht and will then be sailing for several months. It was a well-paid job.

Three days, seventy-two hours, four thousand three hundred and twenty minutes, passed by more quickly than he would have liked, they should say 'goodbye' to each other, but he wasn't capable of doing this.

Early in the morning, he had to take a bus to Spain, and for nearly twenty-four hours, he would be travelling in a dirty dusty vehicle within which there would be twenty things around, that irritated him, though in itself, this wasn't particularly important. It won't be too long now before he was busy with the yacht and will then be sailing for several months. It was a well-paid job.

Jo brought Sasha back to her house, hurriedly kissed her, and after she had got out of the car, he pressed the accelerator pedal, but before turning the corner, took one last look at her in the mirror.

She was standing, with arms folded, near to the house entrance wearing a white T-shirt and simple blue jeans, watching his car disappear. She looked like a small girl with wet hair who had just come from a swimming pool, and right then, he was desperate to cuddle her. Jo applied more pressure to the gas pedal.

It was early morning and the sun hadn't appeared above the roof of the high building that had panoramic views of the seafront.

A young slim girl, with her long hair gathered into a bun, dressed in a white T-shirt, and sports trousers was running along the narrow sandy path part of the route of which was near the perimeter of this building. She was thinking of tomorrow's visit to that well-known eccentric psychoanalyst, Sargun.

She didn't notice whether there was anybody around her and, was running so fast that the small dog walking nearby couldn't follow. It came to a halt on the promenade and stared at her, a young man in a hurry pulled the dog along by its leash several times.

At home, two children were waiting for him to take them to school, and his wife was tired.

'Damn dog', he thought with irritation. *'I was against having this dog, and now, as a result of giving him a home, have to walk him, every day.'*

Grumbling angrily and cringing from the cold wind, he pulled the dog indoors.

Snow-white coloured yacht masts swayed in the wind like the slender trunks of palm trees. Because of bad weather, there was practically nobody at the seaport, and the wind brought heavy rainfall from the mountains. A thick sheet of grey clouds covered the sky.

A young man on one of the yachts looked towards the seashore, frowned, and began to coil the vessel's rope, his hands being covered in blood and his corns had not had time to heal but much work had yet to be completed before 'Destiny' could sail.

People come and people go, that is life. The only difference is that some people can choose to come or go as they please and some have no choice.

We have what we have.

End of story…?

www.ingramcontent.com/pod-product-compliance
Lightning Source LLC
LaVergne TN
LVHW041649060526
838200LV00040B/1774